To the memory of Florrie.
And for Paul, with love and thanks,
for believing and being there.

tiger tales
an imprint of ME Media, LLC
202 Old Ridgefield Road, Wilton, CT 06897
First published in the United States 1998 by Little Tiger Press
This edition published in the United States 2002
Originally published in Great Britain 1998,
By Methuen Children's Books, London
Text and illustrations copyright ©1998 Jan Fernley
CIP data is available
ISBN 1-58925-371-X
Printed in Dubai
1 3 5 7 9 10 8 6 4 2

Little Robin's Christmas

by Jan Fearnley

tiger tales

It was the week before Christmas and Little Robin was getting very excited. He washed and ironed seven warm vests, one for each of the chilly days ahead.

Little Robin put on his white vest
and went to skate on the pond.

On the way he met Frog. "I'm so
cold!" said Frog. "I wish I had a
warm vest."

Little Robin gave Frog his white vest.
"I still have six vests left," thought
Little Robin as Frog thanked him and
hopped off happily.

Six days before Christmas Little Robin put on his green vest and ran out to play in the snow.

Down the path came Hedgehog. "I'm freezing!" he said miserably.

Little Robin gave Hedgehog his green vest.
"I still have five vests left," thought Little Robin,
waving good-bye to his prickly friend.

Five days before Christmas Little Robin put on
his pink vest and set out to hunt for worms.

He had not gone far when Mole
appeared. "Brr!" said Mole. "The ground
is too hard to dig and I'm chilly!"

Little Robin gave his pink vest to
Mole. It was a bit tight, but Mole loved it.
He was nice and warm.

"Four vests left," thought Little Robin.

Four days before Christmas Little
Robin put on his yellow vest and flew to
the tall oak tree, where he met Squirrel.
"I'm so cold I can't sleep!"
Squirrel said with a yawn.

Little Robin handed over his yellow vest.
"Only three vests left now," he thought as
Squirrel thanked him and promptly dozed off.

Three days before Christmas
Little Robin put on his blue vest.

He was swooping down through
the clouds when he saw Rabbit
on a hill.
"I'm so cold my teeth are
chattering!" said Rabbit, shivering.

Little Robin gave Rabbit his blue vest. It made the perfect hat for him.

"Well, I've still got two left," Little Robin said to himself as Rabbit went cheerfully on his way.

Two days before Christmas Little Robin put on his purple vest and hopped along the riverbank.

Next to the river stood Otter with her baby,
who was very unhappy.

"My baby is sick!" said Otter.

Little Robin's purple vest was just right for
Baby Otter and made him feel much better.
"Oh dear," thought Little Robin. "I only have
one vest left."

On Christmas Eve Little Robin put on his
very last vest, a warm orange one. He'd been
walking and whistling to himself for some
time when he met a cold little mouse
huddled in the garden.

Little Robin felt so sorry for her that he took
off his last warm vest and pulled it over her.
"Thank you!" cried the mouse.

Now it was late. The snow was falling
and poor Little Robin had nothing to wear.
There was nobody to help him and it
was a long way back to his nest. He fluffed
up his feathers as best he could and
huddled on a snowy roof.

Soon he fell fast asleep.
Not even the sleigh bells
woke him, or the crunch
of snow under heavy
black boots.

Large hands carefully
picked up Little Robin.
"You had better come
with me, Little Robin,"
chuckled a jolly voice.

The man took him a long way in a sleigh. When he got home, the man said to his wife, "This is the generous little fellow I told you about."

"He must have a very special present then," she replied.

And with Little Robin snug and cozy in her lap, the lady set to work. She pulled a thread from a big red coat, and with it she knitted a tiny vest. It was a perfect fit for the little bird.

"I'm very proud of you," said the man to Little Robin when he woke up. "You gave away all your warm vests to other animals. You are full of the spirit of Christmas."

"I want you to have this vest. It is very special. It will keep you warm forever, and when others see you in it, it will make them feel warm, too."

It was time to go, and the man put Little Robin back into his sleigh. Little Robin was very happy. His chest glowed as red as a reindeer's nose.

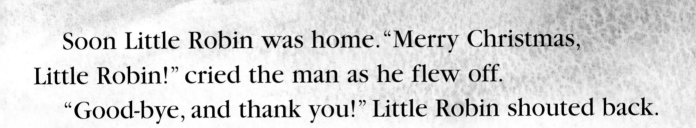

Soon Little Robin was home. "Merry Christmas,
Little Robin!" cried the man as he flew off.
"Good-bye, and thank you!" Little Robin shouted back.

It was Christmas morning. Boys and girls
everywhere were opening their presents.
Little Robin flew to the highest branch of a tree,
proudly wearing his new red vest, and sang out
sweetly, wishing everyone "Merry Christmas!"

1 2 3 4 5
6 7 8 9 10 11
12 13 14